X-TREME FACTS: SPACE

STARS AND GALAXIES

by Catherine C. Finan

Minneapolis, Minnesota

Credits:

Cover, Maxal Tamor/Shutterstock, Antares_StarExplorer/Shutterstock, Klever_ok/Shutterstock, Alter-ego/Shutterstock; Title Page, 7 top, 8, 22 bottom, 23 middle, NASA, ESA, and the Hubble Heritage Team (STScI/AURA)/Public Domain; 4–5, structuresxx/Shutterstock; 4 top, Withan Tor/Shutterstock; 5 top, 6 top, 22 top, 24 top, **NASA/Public Domain; 5 top left, Sergey Nivens/Shutterstock; 5 bottom left, stockyimages/Shutterstock; 5 bottom right, LightField Studios/Shutterstock; 6 bottom, ESA/Public Domain; 7, 19 top, ESA/Creative Commons; 8 bottom right, dekazigzag/Shutterstock; 9 top, Volodymyr Goinyk/Shutterstock; 9, NASA, ESA, and C.R. O'Dell (Vanderbilt University)/Public Domain; 9 bottom right, Stock-Asso/Shutterstock; 10 top right, Pablo Carlos Budassi/Creative Commons; 10 bottom left, 11 bottom left, middle, 17 bottom, Joshua Avramson/Creative Commons; 10 right, Dennis Jarvis/Creative Commons; 11 top, Oona Räisänen/Public Domain; 11 middle, Triff/Shutterstock, sciencepics/Shutterstock; 11 bottom right, Pablo Carlos Budassi/Creative Commons; 12 top, Sahara Prince/Shutterstock; 12 bottom left, djmilic/Shutterstock; 12 bottom right, Prostock-studio/Shutterstock; 13 top, Triff/Shutterstock; 13 top right, 16 top, ESO/M. Kornmesser/Creative Commons; 13 bottom, Tom Wang/Shutterstock; 13 bottom left, Nutlegal Photographer/Shutterstock; 13 bottom right, LightField Studios/Shutterstock; 14 top, vchal/Shutterstock; 14 bottom, 15 top, 15 bottom, Allexxandar/Shutterstock; 15 top right, Vector FX/Shutterstock; 15 bottom left, fizkes/Shutterstock; 15 bottom right, Viacheslav Lopatin/Shutterstock.com; 16–17 bottom, paulista/Shutterstock; 16 bottom right, AstroStar/Shutterstock; 17 top, NASA, ESA, J. Hester and A. Loll (Arizona State University)/Public Domain; 17 middle, 17 bottom left, JhonyCoder/Shutterstock; 18 Alain r/Creative Commons; 19 NRAO/AUI/NSF; Dana Berry/SkyWorks; ALMA (ESO/NAOJ/NRAO)/Creative Commons; 19 bottom right, Roman Samborskyi/Shutterstock; 20 top, Pablo Carlos Budassi /Creative Commons; 20 bottom, Gorodenkoff/Shutterstock; 21, MarcelClemens/Shutterstock; 21 top, NASA, ESA, and M. Brodwin (University of Missouri)/Creative Commons; 21 middle, 27 top, Adam Evans/Creative Commons; 21 bottom left, WeAre/Shutterstock; 21 bottom right, Johan Hagemeyer/Public Domain; 23 bottom, NASA, ESA, and the Hubble Heritage Team (STScI/AURA)-ESA/Hubble Collaboration/Public Domain; 23 top, NASA, ESA, and The Hubble Heritage Team (STScI/AURA); J. Blakeslee (Washington State University)/Public Domain; 24 middle, Vadim Sadovski/Shutterstock; 24 bottom, Marc Imhoff/NASA GSFC, Christopher Elvidge/NOAA NGDC; Image: Craig Mayhew and Robert Simmon/NASA GSFC/Public Domain; 25, Zach Dischner/Creative Commons; 25 bottom, Grand Canyon NPS/Creative Commons; 26 bottom, ESO/Yuri Beletsky/Creative Commons; 26 bottom left, Nanette Dreyer/Shutterstock; 26 bottom right, JuneChalida/Shutterstock; 27 bottom, NASA; ESA; Z. Levay and R. van der Marel, STScI; T. Hallas; and A. Mellinger/Public Domain; 27 bottom right, dotshock/Shutterstock; 28 top, traXX/Shutterstock; 28 bottom left, Scott Heaney/Shutterstock; 28 middle right, Pj Aun/Shutterstock; 28 right lower middle, Chones/Shutterstock; 28–29, Austen Photography, v_zaitsev/iStock

President: Jen Jenson
Director of Product Development: Spencer Brinker
Senior Editor: Allison Juda
Associate Editor: Charly Haley
Designer: Elena Klinkner

Developed and produced for Bearport Publishing by BlueAppleWorks Inc.
Managing Editor for BlueAppleWorks: Melissa McClellan
Art Director: T.J. Choleva
Photo Research: Jane Reid

Library of Congress Cataloging-in-Publication Data

Names: Finan, Catherine C., 1972- author.
Title: Stars and galaxies / by Catherine C. Finan.
Description: Minneapolis, Minnesota : Bearport Publishing Company, [2022] | Series: X-treme facts: space | Includes bibliographical references and index.
Identifiers: LCCN 2021030944 (print) | LCCN 2021030945 (ebook) | ISBN 9781636915128 (library binding) | ISBN 9781636915197 (paperback) | ISBN 9781636915265 (ebook)
Subjects: LCSH: Stars--Juvenile fiction. | Galaxies--Juvenile fiction.
Classification: LCC QB801.7 .F56 2022 (print) | LCC QB801.7 (ebook) | DDC 523.8--dc23
LC record available at https://lccn.loc.gov/2021030944
LC ebook record available at https://lccn.loc.gov/2021030945

Copyright © 2022 Bearport Publishing Company. All rights reserved. No part of this publication may be reproduced in whole or in part, stored in any retrieval system, or transmitted in any form or by any means, electronic, mechanical, photocopying, recording, or otherwise, without written permission from the publisher.

For more information, write to Bearport Publishing, 5357 Penn Avenue South, Minneapolis, MN 55419.
Printed in the United States of America.

Contents

What's Out There? 4
A Very Big Bang 6
You're a Star! 8
From Dwarf to Giant 10
Our Star, the Sun 12
The Constellation Situation 14
Death of a Star 16
Inside a Black Hole 18
Galaxy Gazing 20
Shape Up 22
The Magnificent Milky Way 24
Hey, Neighbor! 26

Constellation Art 28
Glossary 30
Read More 31
Learn More Online 31
Index 32
About the Author 32

What's Out There?

Have you ever looked at a clear night sky and wondered how many stars are up there? It's way too many to count! Those stars twinkling in the darkness are part of the 200 billion stars in our Milky Way **galaxy**. And scientists think there could be 100 billion galaxies in the universe, each with billions of stars. Far out!

The sun is at the center of our solar system. Earth and other planets **orbit** around it.

Our sun is one of the galaxy's many, many stars.

The sun is closer to Earth than other stars, but it's still 93 million miles (150 million km) away.

A Very Big Bang

So, how did these billions of galaxies and their stars form? It all started with what **astronomers** call the Big Bang. About 13.8 billion years ago, the universe exploded out from a tiny speck and formed in less than a second. Then, it kept growing. Eventually, **atoms** of the gases hydrogen and helium formed in the universe. These gases came together to make stars, and the stars grouped together into galaxies.

Before the Big Bang, all **matter** in the universe was inside a tiny point thousands of times smaller than the head of a pin!

In 1929, astronomer Edwin Hubble discovered that the universe was still **expanding** and was much larger than people thought!

Stars and galaxies formed about 200 million years after the Big Bang.

BETTER LATE THAN NEVER!

Modern scientists have used powerful **telescopes** to find ancient gas clouds and light from the beginning of the universe.

ARE YOU READY, GALAXIES? SAY CHEESE!

The Hubble Space Telescope was named after Edwin Hubble. It takes pictures of stars and galaxies.

You're a Star!

Stars are giant balls of hot gases—mostly hydrogen and helium—held together by **gravity**. Most of them form inside clouds of gas and dust called nebulas. But what makes stars glow? They shine as **pressure** inside them turns hydrogen into helium, which makes a lot of energy and light. Stars shine for as long as they have hydrogen **fuel**.

Nebulas are sometimes called star nurseries because stars are born inside them.

The Eagle Nebula is also called the **Pillars** of Creation because it is the birthplace of so many stars.

I'LL MAKE YOU A STAR!

NO, THANKS. I'D RATHER STAY HERE ON EARTH.

The energy and light made at a star's core can take a million years to reach the star's surface and shine out.

From Dwarf to Giant

All stars are big, but some are much bigger than others. In fact, stars come in many sizes, temperatures, and colors! Blue giant stars are among the hottest stars. They are huge and extremely bright. Their hydrogen burns fast, so they might shine for only a few million years. The smallest, coolest stars are called red dwarf stars. Because their hydrogen burns slowly, they last much longer than blue giants.

Red dwarfs are the most common type of star.

Scientists think **red dwarf stars can shine for trillions of years.**

WHY DO YOU BOTHER WITH THAT GIANT STAR? DWARF STARS LAST LONGER!

TO EACH THEIR OWN!

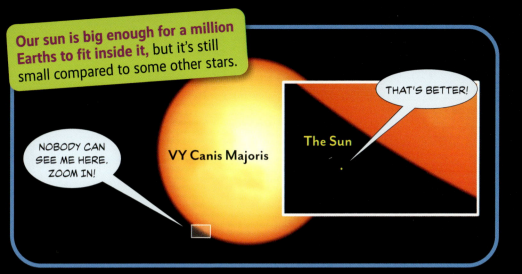

Our sun is big enough for a million Earths to fit inside it, but it's still small compared to some other stars.

NOBODY CAN SEE ME HERE. ZOOM IN!

VY Canis Majoris

THAT'S BETTER!

The Sun

VY Canis Majoris is a red hypergiant star in the Milky Way galaxy. It's so huge, 3 billion suns could fit inside it!

Our sun is a **yellow dwarf star.**

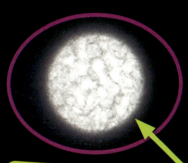

Different-colored stars are different temperatures. Red stars can be as cool as 5,800°F (3,200°C), while the hottest blue stars can be 71,500°F (39,700°C).

Just one teaspoon of material from **a white dwarf star would weigh 100 tons (91 t)!**

Red Star   Yellow Star   Blue Star

Coolest   Hottest

11

Our Star, the Sun

Compared to the countless stars in our galaxy and other galaxies, our sun is just an average-sized yellow dwarf star. Still, there would be no life on Earth without it! That makes the sun a pretty big deal. It holds more than 99 percent of all the **mass**, or the amount of stuff, in our solar system and has a surface temperature of 10,000°F (5,500°C). Not too shabby for an average star!

The sun is middle-aged! It formed 4.6 billion years ago and will shine for another 5 billion years.

I MAY BE MIDDLE-AGED, BUT I'VE STILL GOT A LOT OF ENERGY!

WHAT A CHAMPION! LONG LIVE THE SUN!

Every second, the sun produces as much energy as 100 billion tn. (91 billion t) of exploding **dynamite**.

12

It takes 8 minutes and 20 seconds for light from the sun to reach Earth.

The Constellation Situation

Have you ever thought you could see pictures in the stars? Constellations are groups of stars that look like they form shapes in the night sky. For thousands of years, people have found images they recognize in the stars. Today, there are 88 official constellations. They are often named after characters and creatures from famous stories. Let's look for pictures in the stars!

Orion the Hunter is a constellation that's easy to spot. Just look for the three stars of his belt!

CAN YOU SEE THE BELT?

I CAN SEE THE WHOLE THING!

Canis Major, or the Greater Dog, follows behind Orion. **The brightest star in the night sky, Sirius, is part of this constellation.**

Have you ever seen the Big Dipper? The Big Dipper is not an official constellation by itself, **but it's part of the constellation Ursa Major, which means Great Bear.**

The Little Dipper is officially the constellation Ursa Minor, or Little Bear.

North Star

Big Dipper in Ursa Major

The tip of the Little Dipper's handle is the North Star. Sailors used this star to find their way at sea many years ago.

HEY HERCULES, DO YOU WANT TO GO LOOK FOR CONSTELLATIONS WITH ME?

The constellation Draco is named for **the dragon killed by the Greek hero Hercules.**

SURE, I DON'T MIND LOOKING AT THE STARS. I JUST DON'T LIKE DRAGONS!

Death of a Star

Stars shine for billions or even trillions of years, but they don't shine forever. As stars run out of hydrogen fuel, they become red giants. When the fuel is gone, the stars die. Their deaths can be quiet or dramatic, depending on the star's size. Smaller stars die slowly over time. Huge stars might explode in an event called a supernova. *Boom!*

A star must be at least five times the mass of our sun to explode as a supernova.

Although supernovas are rare, scientists have seen them through telescopes. Supernovas are the biggest explosions ever seen by humans.

The leftover gas from a supernova forms a nebula where more stars may be born!

The Crab Nebula formed after a massive star exploded. Astronomers noticed it almost 1,000 years ago.

Dying stars become red giants because they get cooler as they run out of fuel.

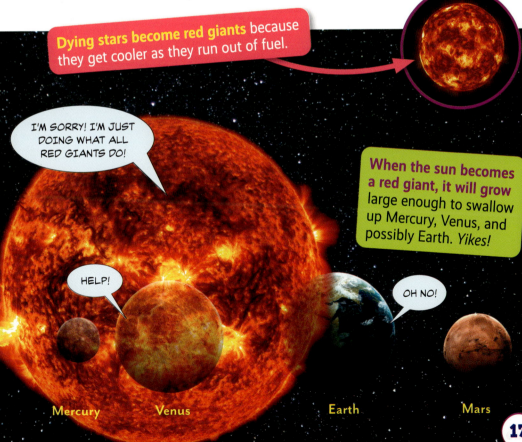

When the sun becomes a red giant, it will grow large enough to swallow up Mercury, Venus, and possibly Earth. *Yikes!*

Mercury   Venus   Earth   Mars

Inside a Black Hole

A star's death can be quite an event. And if the star is supermassive, it might form one of the most mysterious things in the universe—a black hole. We can't see black holes, but we know they exist. How? Because the strong pull of their gravity sucks in nearby space dust, stars, and even entire galaxies! Scientists believe most galaxies have black holes at their centers. Let's shed some light on black holes . . .

A black hole sounds like empty space, **but black holes actually have a huge amount of mass.**

LIGHTS OUT!

The gravity of black holes is so strong that not even light can escape.

The closest black hole to Earth that we know of is still 1,500 **light-years** away. **Scientists nicknamed it The Unicorn!**

Black holes come in different sizes. One of the smallest black holes we know of is only about 15 miles (24 km) across.

Galaxy Gazing

Not so long ago, people believed our galaxy was the only galaxy and that it held all the stars in the universe. Wrong! In 1924, Edwin Hubble discovered a second galaxy called Andromeda. Then, he went on to discover dozens of other galaxies. Now, we know there are billions of galaxies! Each galaxy has billions of stars, as well as plenty of planets, moons, and more.

In every galaxy, stars move around a center point.

I'VE GOT PLACES TO GO AND THINGS TO SEE!

LET'S WATCH THAT GALAXY MOVE!

Galaxies don't stay still. They're constantly moving through space.

Scientists think galaxies are mostly made of what they call dark energy. But they don't know what it is or where it comes from!

Shape Up

There are billions of galaxies, but scientists group them all into just a few main types by their shapes. Spiral galaxies, such as the Milky Way, look a bit like spacey pinwheels. Their stars form giant arms that curl out from the galaxies' centers. Elliptical galaxies are round or oval-shaped, like footballs, with more stars near their centers. Irregular galaxies look like oddly shaped blobs.

Our solar system is located **in a part of the Milky Way called the Orion Arm.**

I'VE BEEN CARRYING THESE STARS FOR A LONG TIME—AND MY ARMS AREN'T EVEN TIRED!

The Sombrero galaxy is a spiral galaxy. Its light shines out in the shape of a hat.

I DON'T WANT TO BE A GALAXY! I WANT TO BE A HAT.

The Magnificent Milky Way

Even though the Milky Way galaxy is shaped like a flat spiral, we see it as a line of white light stretching across the sky. That's because our planet is in the Milky Way, so we are looking at the galaxy from its edge. It was only by studying what we can see from Earth that scientists learned our galaxy is a spiral.

Earth is about halfway between the Milky Way's center and its outer edge.

YOU ARE HERE!

The Milky Way is so huge that light takes 100,000 years to travel from one end to the other.

Many people around the world can't see the Milky Way. The sky needs to be very dark to see it, and many places have too much light from homes, businesses, roads, and more.

Scientists think about **half a dozen new stars are born in the Milky Way each year.**

It takes our solar system 250 million years to orbit the Milky Way's center.

Our galaxy has different names in different languages. The Chinese name for it means silver river, and the Norwegian name means winter way.

LET'S TAKE A CLOSER LOOK AT THE MILKY WAY.

YOU HAVE THE NAME ALL WRONG. IT'S CALLED THE WINTER WAY!

THOSE TWO ARE FUNNY! EVERYBODY KNOWS THAT IT'S CALLED THE SILVER RIVER!

25

Hey, Neighbor!

The Milky Way has neighboring galaxies, but they're much too far away to drop by for a visit! Our galaxy is part of a cluster of galaxies called the Local Group. The group includes small dwarf galaxies, such as Canis Major, as well as the huge Andromeda galaxy. From the galaxies of the Local Group and beyond, the universe is expanding. Scientists think it will keep expanding forever, pulling most galaxies farther and farther apart.

The galaxy closest to us is the Canis Major dwarf galaxy. But it would still take 750 million years for a spacecraft to fly there!

The Milky Way's gravity is slowly ripping Canis Major apart. Sorry, neighbor!

WOW, LOOK AT THAT LASER BEAM REACHING ALL THE WAY TO CANIS MAJOR!

YEAH! I'M GLAD WE GOT TO SEE IT BEFORE IT'S RIPPED APART!

Andromeda is the Milky Way's closest large galaxy neighbor, but it's still 2.5 million light-years away.

I'M COMING FOR YOU, NEIGHBOR!

Andromeda is moving toward the Milky Way at a speed of 70 miles (112 km) per second.

Scientists think the Milky Way and Andromeda will **collide** in 4 billion years.

NOT A CHANCE. I'M STAYING PUT!

MOVE ASIDE, MILKY WAY!

DON'T WORRY, GALAXIES. ACCORDING TO THIS, YOUR CRASH WILL BE PRETTY HARMLESS!

When the Milky Way and Andromeda collide, **scientists think almost no stars or planets will hit one another because galaxies are mostly empty space!**

Constellation Art
Craft Project

The next time you look up at the night sky, see if you can find some pictures in the stars. You can search for the constellations featured in this book or look up others that are easy to spot where you live. Here's a craft to inspire your constellation creation.

What You Will Need

- A picture of a constellation
- A crayon
- Watercolor paper
- Star stickers
- A bowl of water
- A brush
- Watercolor paint
- Salt

The constellations you can see depend on the time of year and where you are.

Step One

Find a picture of a constellation for reference. Using a crayon, write the name of the constellation on the watercolor paper.

Step Two

Referring to the picture as needed, place a star sticker on the paper for each star in the constellation.

Step Three

Paint the whole piece of paper blue. Then, sprinkle some salt around the constellation. The salt will look like little stars around the large constellation. Leave to dry.

Step Four

Carefully remove the star stickers and wipe the salt off of the paper. Your constellation art is complete!

29

astronomers scientists who study the universe beyond Earth

atoms tiny building blocks that make up everything in the universe

collide to crash together

dynamite a strong explosive

expanding becoming larger

fuel something that is burned to make energy and heat

galaxy a collection of billions of stars and other matter held together by gravity

gravity the force that pulls things toward Earth, the sun, or other bodies in space

light-years units that measure the distance light travels in one year

mass the amount of matter in an object

matter all things that contain atoms and take up space

orbit to move in a path around another object; the path is also called an orbit

pillars tall poles used to support a building or structure

pressure the force produced by pressing on something

telescopes instruments that use lenses and mirrors to make distant objects appear larger

Read More

Finan, Catherine C. *Planets and Moons (X-treme Facts: Space).* Minneapolis: Bearport Publishing, 2022.

Rathburn, Betsy. *Galaxies (Torque: Space Science).* Minneapolis: Bellwether Media, 2019.

Wilberforce, Bert. *Black Holes (A Look at Space Science).* New York: Gareth Stevens Publishing, 2021.

Learn More Online

1. Go to **www.factsurfer.com** or scan the QR code below.

2. Enter **"Stars and Galaxies"** into the search box.

3. Click on the cover of this book to see a list of websites.

Index

Andromeda Galaxy 20–21, 26–27

Big Bang 6–7

Big Dipper 15

black holes 18–19

blue giant stars 10

Earth 4–5, 11–13, 17–18, 21, 24

elliptical galaxies 22–23

gravity 8, 18–19, 26

helium 6, 8

Hubble, Edwin 6–7, 20–21

hydrogen 6, 8, 10, 16

irregular galaxies 22–23

Little Dipper 15

Milky Way Galaxy 4–5, 11, 19, 21–22, 24–27

nebulas 8–9, 17

Orion Arm 22

Orion the Hunter 14

red dwarf stars 10

Sagittarius A* 19

spiral galaxies 22, 24

sun 4, 11–13, 16–17

supernovas 16–17

yellow dwarf stars 11–12

About the Author

Catherine C. Finan is a writer living in northeastern Pennsylvania. One of her most-prized possessions is a telescope that lets her peer into space.